SHOW · ME · BOOKS

Chase that Pig!

A STORY IN RHYME WITH THINGS TO FIND

BY MARCIA LEONARD
PICTURES BY MAXIE CHAMBLISS

A BANTAM LITTLE ROOSTER BOOK

TORONTO · NEW YORK · LONDON · SYDNEY · AUCKLAND

For Barbara Miller Hoppe.
—M.L.

For Sarah and Morgan,
my Yorkshire beauties.
—M.C.

CHASE THAT PIG!

A Bantam Book / November 1988

Produced by Small Packages, Inc.

"Bantam Little Rooster" is a trademark of Bantam Books.

Library of Congress Cataloging-in-Publication Data

Leonard, Marcia.
  Chase that pig!

  (Show me books)
  Summary: A rhyming text follows a rambunctious pig
fleeing its bath and asks readers to point out or find
various things in the illustrations.
  [1. Pigs—Fiction. 2. Literary recreations.
3. Stories in rhyme] I. Chambliss, Maxie, ill.
II. Title. III. Series: Leonard, Marcia. Show me books.
PZ8.3.L54925Ch 1988   [E]   88-3421
ISBN 0-553-05476-7

Published simultaneously in the United States and Canada

Bantam Books are published by Bantam Books, a division of Bantam
Doubleday Dell Publishing Group, Inc. Its trademark, consisting of the
words "Bantam Books" and the portrayal of a rooster, is Registered in U.S.
Patent and Trademark Office and in other countries. Marca Registrada.
Bantam Books, 666 Fifth Avenue, New York, New York 10103.

PRINTED IN THE UNITED STATES OF AMERICA

RM   0 9 8 7 6 5 4 3 2 1

One sunny day in summer, on a farm just outside town,
Christine and Claire O'Reilly gave their pig a scrubbing down.
To find out how this bathtime turned into a crazy spree,
just read the rhymes that follow and then tell me what you see.

The girls had entered Peachy in the local county fair.
They hoped she'd win a ribbon, so they groomed her with great care.
But Peach was feeling frisky. She caught both those girls off guard!
And, dashing from her pigpen, she escaped into the yard.

Chase that pig!

Look closely at this picture and then point out what you see.
Find the horses in the barn and the cows beneath the tree.
Find the hens and all their chicks, find the lambs and woolly ewe.
Find the rooster on the fence, who says COCK-A-DOODLE-DO!

What other animals do you see?

The piggy had a head start, but Christine and Claire were quick.
They caught Peach near the farmhouse, only she was wet and slick!
She wriggled from their fingers. She was on the move once more—
colliding with the laundry that was hanging by the door.

Grab that pig!

Look closely at this picture. Do you see a checkered shirt?
Two brightly colored dresses, and a polka-dotted skirt?
Now find some striped pajamas that belong to Mr. O',
a pair of purple knee socks, and a nightgown with a bow.

What else can you find?

While Claire and Chris were struggling to undo what Peach had done,
she trotted to the workshed, looking for some brand-new fun.
She spotted Pete O'Reilly, who was fixing up his bike,
and politely asked him OINK? but he only answered YIKE!

Catch that pig!

Look closely at this picture and please show me if you can,
a clock in need of mending and a broken down old fan.
Now show me three screwdrivers and a hammer with some nails,
a saw, a pair of pliers, and a paintbrush with some pails.

What else can you show me?

Once all the wash was rescued, Claire and Chris resumed the chase.
So Peachy left the farmyard at a very rapid pace!
Then as she hit the main road, that fat pig smelled something grand.
In seconds she was lunching at the neighbors' produce stand.

What a greedy pig!

Look closely at this picture. There is so much here to eat!
What is piled up in the bins? What is next to Peach's feet?
Look for cucumbers and corn, look for cherries ripe and red.
Find potatoes, plums, and pears, and some loaves of homemade bread.

What other fruits and vegetables do you recognize?

Peach swallowed one last mouthful as the girls drew near the stand,
then hurried off toward Main Street, where she spied a marching band.
She didn't even notice the impression that she made,
and following the tubas, she marched off with the parade!

Follow that pig!

Look closely at this picture of a band that's passing by.
See the trumpets and the flute and the banner held so high?
See the shiny slide trombones and the tiny piccolos.
See the prancing majorette, who is marching on her toes.

What else do you see?

The band marched right down Main Street to the entrance of the fair,
with Peachy and the tubas followed close by Chris and Claire.
Then Peach sat on the platform while the mayor gave a speech—
in view of *all* the people, but—of course—just out of reach.

Oh, that pig!

Look closely at this picture, at the people short and tall.
Find a man who's very large and a child who's very small.
Find some people wearing hats and some more with glasses on.
Find a girl with long red hair and a man whose hair is gone.

What else can you point to?

Peach thought the speech was boring, and she soon made up her mind
to take leave of these humans and to seek out her own kind.
When Claire and Chris next saw her, they could not believe their eyes.
The lady judging livestock had just given Peach FIRST PRIZE!

What a perfect pig!

Look closely at this picture. It's a piggy jamboree!
First count the reddish brown pigs, then the pink pigs that you see.
Count piggies that are spotted and black pigs that have white bands.
Then count up all the children who have ribbons in their hands.

What else can you count?

The county fair is over; the O'Reilly girls are home.
They've put Peach in a pasture, where she has some room to roam.
And on her private pigpen they have written—very big—
"You may be rather naughty, but you're one PEACH of a pig!"